Fionn Mac Cumhail's
Epic Adventures

Eddie Lenihan

Illustrated by Alan Clarke

MERCIER PRESS

Cork

www.mercierpress.ie

© Text: Eddie Lenihan, 2015

Stories adapted from *Irish Tales of Mystery and Magic,*
published by Mercier Press in 2006.

© Illustrations: Alan Clarke

Produced for Mercier Press by Teapot Press Ltd

Abridged and edited by Fiona Biggs
Designed by Alyssa Peacock & Tony Potter

ISBN: 978-1-78117-358-9

10 9 8 7 6 5 4 3 2 1

A CIP record for this title is available from the British Library

Printed and bound in China

CONTENTS

෩⊚෨ ෩⊚෨

Taoscán Mac Liath and the Magic Bees

෩⊚෨ ෩⊚෨

How the First Blackbird came to Ireland

෩⊚෨ ෩⊚෨

Pronunciation guide

Taoscán Mac Liath
and the
Magic Bees

King Cormac spends a lot on honey, and is delighted when his druid comes across some magic bees. But when things go badly wrong, Fionn Mac Cumhail comes to the rescue.

Long ago, people had no sweetener except honey – there was no sugar at all in those days.

At that time most of the honey in Ireland was produced in Clonmel. The honey man was called Mel and he had a huge field crammed with hives. Mel made so much money out of his honey that he was almost as rich as King Cormac himself.

But then something happened. The king's druid, Taoscán Mac Liath, went off, as usual, to the annual druids' conference. At the conference a druid from Iceland, called Baldur, lectured them on all sorts of things, from the cure for carbuncles to the best fish oil for squeaky chariot wheels.

And then he began the last part of his speech, all about bees. They all sat up and listened when he said that 'though there are not many flowers in Iceland, ve have got secret to produce honey in big much from small land.'

Taoscán knew that if he could learn that secret and take it back to King Cormac it would save Cormac a fortune, so he was sure to be pleased.

Just before dinner Taoscán cornered Baldur. He had the friendliest chat imaginable with him and it wasn't long before all the secret's in Baldur's head were safely in his own.

When Taoscán got home he went into his cave without speaking to anyone and barred the door. The day wore on, and at last King Cormac knocked at the door of the cave. 'Taoscán! Are you sick or what?'

No sound for a minute. Cormac was just about to lose his temper when he heard, 'Bzzzzzz.'

Then the door swung open and 'BZZZZZZZ!' – out roared a swarm of bees. They thundered off in a cloud over the Hill of Tara.

'Bless and protect us!' gasped Cormac, 'where did they come from?'

'Oh-ho-ho!' chuckled Taoscán. 'Come in 'til I show you.'

'Well?' said Cormac, 'what is it you have for me?'

'This,' replied Taoscán, holding up a small bag, very like the money bags that travelling men hung

about their necks at that time, 'is for the bees. They're living in that bag, and I can call them back here any time I want to.'

'Do it now, so, 'til I see,' said Cormac, wonder in his voice.

Taoscán took a little whistle from somewhere under his cloak, blew two blasts on it and the swarm of bees roared back into the cave. Then, one by one, into the bag they dropped, thousands upon thousands of them.

'We'll have honey from this day out like no honey in the land of Ireland!' smiled Taoscán.

Every morning from then on Cormac sent two men to Taoscán's cave to bring up the honey on their backs – all out of the small bag, with no trace of a hive or anything else.

One night Fionn said to Cormac, 'Isn't it awful foolishness to be getting our honey still from Mel, when we have our own?'

'I know,' Cormac agreed, 'but we're doing business with him a long time and I don't like to finish it off without a good reason.'

'Leave it to me,' smiled Fionn.

He went down to the storeroom where the barrels of honey were kept, opened one of two barrels there, stirred in a fistful of dried herbs, put on the cover again and left, smiling.

Three weeks later, at a very important feast, the sweetened wine was brought in, made from the honey in the two barrels. Everyone who drank the doctored honey-drink had to be excused early, bent double from cramps and pains.

King Cormac was very embarrassed.

'Here,' said Fionn, pushing his goblet over to the king, 'what do you make of that?' Cormac tasted it. It was unsweetened wine, and perfectly good.

'Ho!' roared Cormac, putting two and two together. 'That villain Mel. His honey was off. Cancel our order with him this very night!'

Before dawn a messenger was riding hard towards Clonmel to give Mel the bad news that the king had his own honey, and the best, too!

And so the fame of the bees of Tara spread. Things soon got so bad for Mel that his business began to fail. One night he sat down with his wife and his three sons and said, 'There'll be no living for any one of the three of you if something isn't done about those bees above in Tara!'

'Don't worry,' said
Maolruan, the youngest
son. 'I'll go to Tara and
I won't come home with
my hands empty.'

'Good lad,' said Mel,
'we are all depending
on you.'

He set out for Tara that very night and arrived
at the foot of the hill just as the sun was rising.

He planted himself in a shady spot, high enough
to give him a clear view of all the country around
and waited. Just before sunset, his keen eyes picked
out a cloud of bees lumbering heavily towards Tara.

His eyes locked on the bees and followed them
all the way to their destination – Taoscán's cave.
As he watched, they streamed in through a little
window in the side of the cave and vanished from
his sight. He darted to the cave, hunching his
shoulders low. He peeped in the window but saw no
trace of the bees. Stranger still, he saw no hive.

If only he had seen the bag hanging down by the
window he could have put in his hand and taken it,
but how could he have known that the bees were
in it?

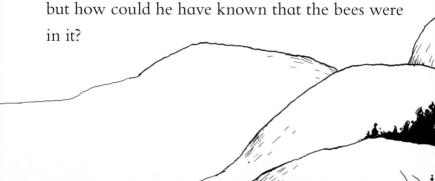

He stepped round to the front door and knocked. Taoscán came out.

'I need help,' said Maolruan. 'Is there a druid in these parts? My brother and myself were travelling to Tara when his horse threw him near where the stream crosses the road. He can't get up and I'm afraid something is broken.'

'Hold on until I get my bag,' said Taoscán. 'Take me to the place.'

'Would you mind if I stayed here? I have a weak stomach for injuries,' said Maolruan.

Taoscán gave him a look, but went off alone, pulling closed the door after him without locking it. As soon as he was out of sight Maolruan dived into the cave and rooted around, but could find no trace of any bees.

Glancing out the window, he saw Taoscán hurrying back. Just as was turning from the window he saw the bag, snatched it and ran for the door. Just in time! Taoscán stomped up, muttering and growling to himself. Maolruan hid at one side until he heard the door closing, then ran down the hill and off towards Clonmel.

Taoscán only discovered the robbery the following morning. 'My bees are gone!' he wailed. 'What's to be done?'

Then he shook himself, poked up the fire to get the smoke rising and then added a pinch of vision-powder. Immediately in the smoke he saw Maolruan running along a road near Clonmel, the stolen bag dangling from his belt.

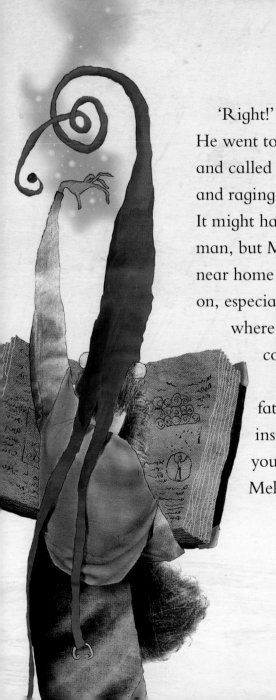

'Right!' said Taoscán.
He went to his spell-book
and called down black clouds
and raging winds on Maolruan.
It might have stopped another
man, but Maolruan was very
near home now, so he struggled
on, especially since he guessed
where the storm was
coming from.

He made it to his
father's house and ran
inside, panting. 'Did
you get the bees?'
Mel asked.

'I couldn't find them,' stuttered Maolruan.
'I saw them going into his cave, but there was
no sign of them when I went in, not even their
hive. But I got his money.'

'What *ráiméis* are you talking? Bees without
a hive?' Mel snatched the purse from Maolruan,
and swung it to hit his son over the head.

'Sure, there's nothing in this purse, you
simpleton!'

He pulled the string of the purse in his temper,
and as soon as he did he heard the 'Bzzzzz!'
He snapped it shut and in an instant his whole
face changed.

'D'you realise what's in this bag, here?'
Mel asked.

'No,' said the three sons.

'The bees. The bees! Shhh! Listen.'

He loosened the string of the purse, and ...
'Bzzzz!'

'Aha!' laughed Mel. 'We'll win this battle. All we have to do is keep these lads in the bag and soon Cormac and all our old customers will have to come to us again. But, they'll pay well for their honey this time! We'll double the price and halve the supply.'

There was just one problem: Mel and his sons weren't used to managing magic bees, so they decided to put the bag down behind the bed and to forget about it. But all the time the bees were busy inside the bag and when no one was taking out the honey or when they couldn't get out to stretch themselves, naturally enough the bag was expanding, although it was a magic bag so it couldn't actually burst. So it stretched and stretched until it filled the room. It was only when the family were going to bed that they discovered what was happening and by then it was too late to do anything.

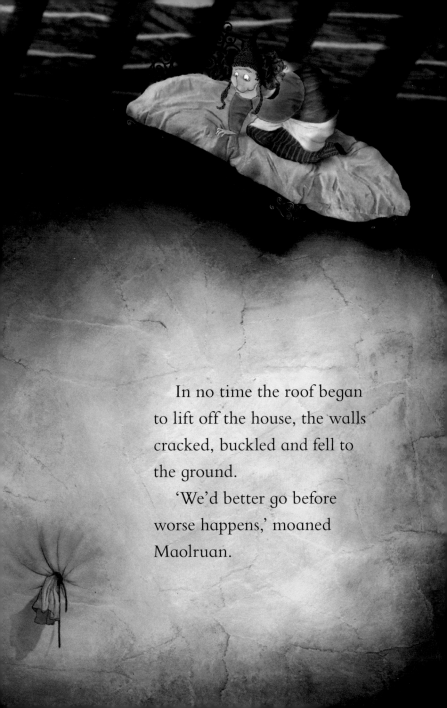

In no time the roof began
to lift off the house, the walls
cracked, buckled and fell to
the ground.

'We'd better go before
worse happens,' moaned
Maolruan.

'And if they get out and follow us?' snarled Mel.
'No! We'll have to get that druid fellow from Tara
down here to control them. Maolruan, go back
and see can you persuade him to come.'

Maelruan set off, protesting all the way. But he
never got to Tara, because a mile down the road
he heard marching feet coming in his direction.

Then, before he could make up his mind to run, he saw the Fianna bearing down on him, fully armed and led by Fionn and Taoscán.

Maolruan fell on his knees, begged their forgiveness and their help all in the one breath, and was starting to explain about the terrible bag when Fionn silenced him: 'Don't be telling us what we know already! Taoscán Mac Liath followed it all in the smoke, and lucky for you that he did. Get up at once, and lead on home!'

When they marched into the yard of Mel's house they saw the strangest sight ever, what looked like an overgrown bladder swelling and growing where the house used to be. Mel stepped out from behind a bush and said to Taoscán: 'Wise man, we did wrong and we know it! But make allowance for our foolishness. Just take away the bees and we'll do whatever you say.'

Taoscán thought Mel had
suffered enough so he said: 'In
spite of your wrongdoing, I'll take
this no further. But you'll ...'

Just then there was a loud
commotion behind them,
and there was King Cormac
himself, springing from his
chariot, striding towards
them.

'Well, now,' said he, 'are
you still standing here looking at
each other? Get that honey out of
there, and don't spill a drop. Jump
to it! I have important guests
coming tonight.'

Fionn hesitated, lost for ideas. He looked hopefully at Taoscán.

'I'll try my spell-books,' he said, 'but I'm nearly sure I have no spells for bees.'

He was right. He had none. Just then Mel jumped up and said to his sons, 'Run to the barrel-shed and get the big tap!'

Maolruan came running back, tap in hand, and Mel set to work, whistling to himself all the while.

He took the tap to the neck of the bag and began to talk to himself, as the bystanders thought.

'Where are you? Come on out, now. You're going home.'

'Look at the bag,' breathed Fionn. The bag had stopped growing and all the heaving inside had quietened. Mel beckoned to Taoscán.

'They want to go home,' he stated.

'Who wants to go home?' asked Taoscán.

'The bees! The bees, of course! I'm talking here to the queen, and she just told me that they're lonesome for Iceland and they want to go back.'

'No such thing!' yelled Taoscán.

At those words a buzzing that sounded like a scream rose from inside and the bag began to swell again, twice as fast as before.

'Oh! Now you upset her. We're all doomed now, 'cos when the bag bursts they'll follow us to the four corners of the world,' moaned Mel.

'Is there any other cure but to let them off home?' asked Cormac.

'I'm afraid there isn't, your highness,' said Mel.

Cormac sighed. 'Then do what you have to, my good man.'

Mel set to work again and by a mixture of *plámás,* begging and promises he got the queen bee's attention. The bag stopped growing. Mel turned

and said to the crowd, 'The bees are lonesome for home. Surely, men, no fair-minded person would be prepared to stand in their way?'

'No! No, indeed!' shouted a fair section of the crowd.

'So,' he said loudly, 'we'll do the decent thing and let them go. And now, who's first for honey the like of which was never before tasted?'

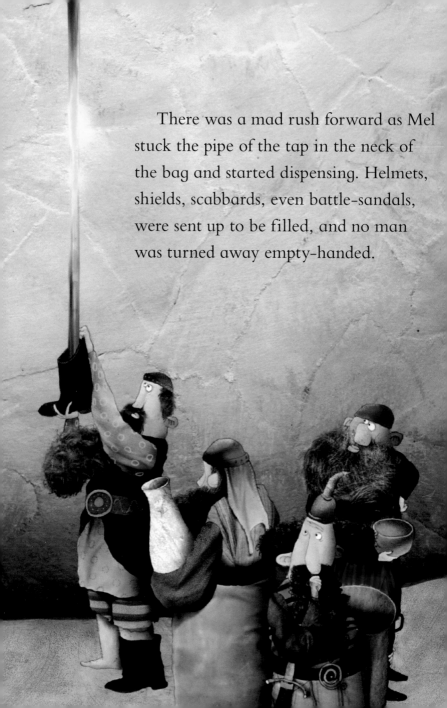

There was a mad rush forward as Mel stuck the pipe of the tap in the neck of the bag and started dispensing. Helmets, shields, scabbards, even battle-sandals, were sent up to be filled, and no man was turned away empty-handed.

On Cormac's orders, the big barrels were brought from Tara and all through the night the work went on. Then silence fell. Even the guards placed on the bag by Fionn slept. Mel crept up to the mouth of the bag, opened the cord carefully and called the bees out. They came in their hundreds and thousands and gathered all over the bag. Mel buzzed his final goodbyes to the queen and went back to bed.

The next morning the guards jumped up as soon as they realised that the bag was gone! Taoscán was called, and he it was who broke the news to Cormac.

'Get Mel and bring him before me at once!' shouted Cormac.

'Tell me!' demanded Cormac. 'Are you good at mixing honey?'

'None better,' replied Mel proudly.

'Good, because I'm appointing you Honey Blender to the High King. Go down to the cellars and put together the right mix of our grand Iceland honey with the ordinary stuff, to make the special honey last as long as possible.'

'I'll need to get a supply of ordinary honey, your highness,' said Mel, winking at Taoscán.

A short while later Maolruan set up his own honey business and he made a success of it in a short time. The orders from Tara grew and grew after Mel discovered that no matter how small an amount of the special honey was mixed with no matter how big an amount of Maolruan's honey the quality remained pure magic!

Father and son prospered. They had honour as well as wealth, and no one was any the wiser about how easy Mel's job really was.

How the First Blackbird came to Ireland

Fionn is tricked by the druids into travelling to Norway to bring blackbirds back to Tara – but he has the last laugh when they sing more sweetly for him than for anyone else.

In the days long ago there was one thing that every man had to be able to do when he was invited to a feast, and that was to stand up and entertain the lord of the house and the other guests. Every chief had his bard and harpist, of course, but the rest of the amusement during and after the feast had to be provided by those who had been invited.

Now, one night, Fionn and three of his men, Goll Mac Mórna, Diarmaid Ó Duibhne and Conán Maol, were travelling the roads of Ireland. They were jumping from pothole to pothole along a winding boreen, when suddenly, out of the gloom ahead, they saw a light coming from a *dún*. They approached the massive wooden door and rapped on it loudly.

When the people inside saw who was there, they welcomed them in, saying, 'Come in, come in!' Fionn and the others entered and sat down, food was brought, the feast went on and the music started. The man with the harp played sweet tunes, but then his fingers got sore and his voice hoarse. The chief called on Fionn to get up and do something to keep the crowd happy.

At once Fionn stood up, settled himself in the middle of the floor and began to recite a long poem. He kept the feasters laughing and crying in turn for two solid hours, and when he stopped they shouted for 'More! More! More!' but Fionn said, 'Hold on! Give my voice a chance. Let someone else take up for a while.'

Diarmaid was next to be chosen. The onlookers asked him to do some mighty deed of strength there and then. Catching the straps of his own sandals, 'NNNNNGGHHH!' he lifted himself up into the air to the height of a man's shoulder.

The feasters clapped him until their hands grew sore, then called the servants to fill the goblets to relieve the excitement.

Then Conán stood out, bowed, and began to sing a sweet, soothing song, in a voice that was neither loud nor rough – a wonderful thing in a man who was very loud and rough.

Goll Mac Mórna was on the point of being called to do his piece when 'BANG! BANG! BANG!' a loud knocking was heard.

When the door was opened, in stepped an old man with a grey cloak wrapped tightly about him. He walked slowly up the hall, and halted before the chief's seat at the top table, bowed down to him and said: 'I claim my right, as a traveller this night.'

'And what might that be?' asked the chief.

'A small bite to eat and a fist of straw in the corner, if you can spare as much, good sir.'

'You're welcome! You're welcome!' said the chief, and he ordered two servants to bring the old man something to eat.

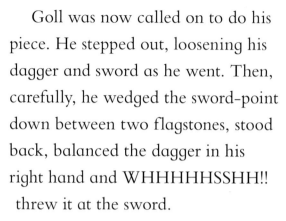

Goll was now called on to do his piece. He stepped out, loosening his dagger and sword as he went. Then, carefully, he wedged the sword-point down between two flagstones, stood back, balanced the dagger in his right hand and WHHHHHSSHH!! threw it at the sword.

It hit the sword at the dead centre of the handle, flashed back, and in that fraction of a second Goll stepped nimbly aside, opened his mouth and snatched it out of the air with his teeth. He bowed to the crowd, smiled, collected his sword and sat down.

The roof and walls shook with the mighty
sound of clapping hands and stomping feet.
It was like thunder. Deafening!

'Well, now,' said the chief, after the noise had
died down and everyone had had another drink,
'we were forgetting about yourself, my good fellow,'
looking in the direction of the old man.

'Come out here, now, and do something for us.
Anything that takes your fancy at all.'

The old man made no stir to get up. He looked
very frightened.

'No insult meant to the house, but I'm no good
in front of a crowd,' said he.

'Is it trying to destroy the old custom and disturb
our whole feast you are?' snarled the lord. 'What
would you like him to do, men?' he cried.

'Whistle!' shouted someone, and the whole
hall took up the cry, 'Whistle! Whistle! Whistle!'

while they hammered the tables with
their daggers and fists. The old man
looked like a hunted hare now, not
knowing which way to turn. 'I can't
whistle!' he protested, 'I can't do
it, I tell you!'

'So, you can't whistle, hmm.
Are you refusing to do it?'
asked the chief grimly.

'No! No, I'm not!' croaked
the old man. 'But look!'
– he opened his
mouth wide –
'Not a tooth
in my head!
How could I
whistle with
them two
bare gums?'

'Whistle! Whistle! Whistle!' chanted the crowd.

'Take him out there to the carpenter,' the chief ordered, 'and he'll hammer a few timber pegs into his jaws an' they'll do for teeth.'

'Nooo! No! No!' wailed the old man, and he made a frantic rush for the door. But the two guards standing there crossed their spears in his path and barred his escape. Fionn rose. This had gone far enough.

'Hold everything, there,' he said smoothly, stepping forward. He had never liked to see the old or the weak mocked.

'Since this man can't whistle like you asked him to, can't you let his place be taken by someone else?'

'Well,' said the chief, doubtfully. 'It would have to be someone very special.'

'Special is what it'll be,' promised Fionn. 'I'll be back in three weeks with something the likes of which you've never heard before.'

Fionn and his three companions left the house, with the old man following them.

'You're no ordinary travelling man,' said Fionn to the old man. 'And you remind me of someone.'

'I'm on my way to see my brother, Taoscán Mac Liath,' explained the stranger.

'That's it!' said Fionn. 'Sure, you're the spit
of him! Come with us and we'll take you to him.'

'I'm a druid myself and I know where he is,'
said the old man.

'A druid, is it!' said Fionn. 'So why couldn't
you do the bit of whistling, then? A fine mess
I'm in now because of you!'

'Acting for a crowd was never a part of
my studies, and I'm not about to learn it now,'
replied the druid. There was something touchy in
his voice as he said it.

'Surely there was some place you could have
pulled a few notes out of, a man of your power?'
burst out Fionn. 'What'll I do now?'

'Maybe there's more to this than you can see yet. We'll go on to Tara and see my brother first thing, that's what we'll do!' snapped the druid, leaving Fionn more mystified than before.

They walked on, arriving at Taoscán's cave at dawn.

Taoscán was up and about already, whistling like a lark as he prepared his breakfast. At the sound of the opening door he turned and an expression of surprise and delight spread over his wrinkled old face. Three steps forward and the brothers were hugging, then they were talking over each other, catching up on all their news.

'Look!' interrupted Fionn, 'Did your brother tell you what I have to do?'

'Don't I know it all,' said Taoscán. 'I was keeping an eye on you in the smoke of my fire. I saw the whole thing.'

'But can you help me now?' asked Fionn.

'Better still,' replied Taoscán, 'You could help yourself. You know your power, Fionn,' he said wearily. At once Fionn brightened up.

'Well! I forgot entirely about it,' he smiled. He put his left hand into the oxter-bag hanging under his right armpit and a needle jabbed itself into his thumb. He jerked the thumb out and straight into his mouth. It was the same thumb he had burned on the Salmon of Knowledge, so the instant he put it into his mouth he saw a vision rise in front of his eyes, a vision of a very stormy sea. Out beyond that ocean he could see land, with forests towering up out of it. Then he thought he heard the sweetest whistling ever heard by human ears, but it was a long way off and he could hear it only in snatches because the gusting wind was whipping it away.

In a little while the vision faded and Fionn came
back to himself. 'Taoscán, what land was that?'

'Oh,' said Taoscán, 'that's the land of Norway.
And that's the place you'll have to go in order to
get the greatest whistlers in the whole world.'

'And what class of a thing was it that I heard
whistling so beautifully?'

'That was *lon dubh*, the blackbird, the very one
that you must bring back to Ireland.'

Fionn set off at a fierce pace for the Giant's
Causeway. A storm was on the sea, just as in
the vision.

He dived straight in and off he went. For two
days he swam, his huge arms never stopping until
he came to the rocky shores of Norway. He hauled
himself up onto the black slippery rocks and set
off along the king's highway.

Before he knew it he was standing before a great royal fort of bright stone, with silver-studded oak doors. He banged on the thick timber with the *Gae Dearg*, his battle-spear. The door was opened and he was let in. He explained his task to the king.

'Oho! We have the very thing you are looking for, the *lon dubh*,' laughed King Olaf. He led Fionn to the top wall of the fort. 'There in the wood you will find him, together with all his family and friends. Take as many of them as you like.'

Fionn was shown out and he rushed off to the forest. He had hardly stepped under the dark green branches when he heard a delicate whistling over his head. He crept up close to the tree, and there above him was perched a jet-black bird with a yellow beak, and another above that again on a higher branch.

He edged his way up the tree until he reached the branch where the first bird was. Slowly he inched his hand towards it. Further and further he stretched his fingers but the bird always skipped just out of range. Then he had an idea. He groped around in the oxter-bag and pulled out a net.

He flung it in the birds' direction and it flew through the air, growing bigger and bigger, spreading wider and wider, until it covered the whole tree where the birds were perched. Fionn pulled it down, took hold of the birds, and stuffed the net back into the oxter-bag. Then he steered himself towards the sea and home.

He soon reached the shore, the birds trembling in his grasp.

'What'll I do now? I can't swim with these lads in my hands.'

He took off his helmet to allow his brain to cool, and an idea came to him. Why not put the birds into the helmet, clamp it back on his head and tie it securely with two plaits of his long hair?

With a short prayer, he waded from the shore and was soon beating down the waves on his way back to Ireland. At the Giant's Causeway he climbed ashore and set off towards Tara. When he got there he hurried up to the king's private chambers.

Neither Cormac nor Fionn was seen again until nightfall. Locked away they were, listening to the birds singing for hours on end.

At the feast that night everyone was in a frenzy of excitement because word had gone about that Fionn had indeed brought back the best whistlers in all the world and that nothing like them had ever been heard before. The occasion was marked by Cormac in brand-new robes, Fionn wearing his best golden helmet.

All were seated and the feast began. But little was eaten and the excitement was mighty.

At last, Fionn raised his hand and lifted the golden helmet. Everyone stared, their mouths open, for there, nestling in Fionn's hair, were four delicate blue eggs.

Fionn put up his hand, but froze at a shout from Taoscán, 'Stop! Don't you see what's after happening? They have their nest made above in your hair.'

'How am I going to get a wink of sleep with them up there?'

'Sleep?' said Taoscán. 'There'll be no more bed until the four eggs are hatched out. Myself and my brother had enough trouble getting those eggs here.'

So it had all been a plot laid by the clever druids!

For almost two weeks Fionn slept on a chair with a guard standing at each side to make sure he did not collapse in the night.

As soon as the four eggs were hatched the nest was carefully removed and Fionn set off down the road with the two birds in his helmet to keep his promise. When he released them on the table in front of the chief they began to sing. The men at the tables were so delighted that they even forgot to eat.

After exactly three minutes Fionn picked up
the birds and replaced them under his helmet.
The chief started to protest, but Fionn said, 'The
promise I made here is kept. If that doesn't satisfy
you, talk to King Cormac.'

And so he left them.

The baby birds grew and grew and in no time
Tara was the envy of all Ireland for sweet song.
Blackbirds eventually swarmed around it in their
thousands, and around Fionn Mac Cumhail
too. For him they sang in a very special way, as
though he were closely related to them. And in
a way, one could say he was, since it was he
who brought them to Ireland in the first place.

Pronunciation guide

Conán Maol – cunnawn mweel

Cormac – core mack

Diarmaid Ó Duibhne – dearmwid oh divna

Fianna – feeanna

Fionn Mac Cumhail – finn mack cool

Gae Dearg – gay darreg

Goll Mac Mórna – gull mack morna

Lon Dubh – lunn duv

Maolruan – mael rooann

Plámás – plawmaws (flattery)

Ráiméis – rawmaysh (nonsense)

Taoscán Mac Liath – tayscawn mack leeah